BITCOIN MONEY

A Tale of Bitville Discovering Good Money

Written by Michael Caras

Illustrated by Marina Yakubivska

Author: Michael Caras
www.thebitcoinrabbi.com
thebitcoinrabbi@gmail.com

Editor: Leah Caras
Design & Layout: Leah Caras
www.carasmaticdesign.com
leah@carasmaticdesign.com

Illustrator: Marina Yakubivska
behance.net/oftennice
marinayakubivska@gmail.com

First Printing, 2019

ISBN 978-0-578-49067-0

Disclaimer:
This book is a fictional allegory for educational and entertainment purposes only. All characters
and events are complete fiction. Nothing in this book should be considered as financial advice or a
recommendation to invest in or purchase any asset.

To my children,
for whom I hope to be making
a brighter, better world.

AUTHOR'S NOTE

Many have heard of the world's first decentralized digital currency, Bitcoin, but few understand how it works and why it was created.

In this short story we explore the origins of money, the invention of Bitcoin, and the role it serves as sound, reliable money.

I believe that the key value of Bitcoin is its economic role, and so we focus on that aspect, as opposed to a detailed explanation of the technology behind it.

Although it appears as a simple children's story, I hope that this book can serve as an introduction to Bitcoin for people of all ages.

I. TRADE

The town of Bitville was filled with children who each had a unique skill. Every kid knew that they could offer something special that other children would want.

"My lemonade is everyone's favorite drink," said Alice. "Maybe I should open a lemonade stand!"

"My father always asks me to mow the lawn because I make the lines straight," Bobby added. "I bet other people would like their lawns mowed, too."

Charlie looked up from his sketchbook. "My friends ask me to make pictures for them because I'm good at drawing."

At first, everyone was happy to trade their own good or service directly for what another person had to offer.

Bobby would mow Alice's lawn in exchange for lemonade.

When Alice wanted a new drawing, she traded lemonade for one of Charlie's pictures.

But one day, things didn't work out so well.

"Bobby, will you mow my lawn for a drawing today?" Charlie asked.

"I don't need any drawings today. I would rather have a lemonade," said Bobby.

However, Alice's lemonade stand was closed because she was at the beach.

Problems like this kept happening. Sometimes Alice wanted her lawn mowed. That would cost five cups of lemonade, but she only had three cups left.

Sometimes Bobby wanted a drawing from Charlie, but Charlie's grass didn't need to be mowed yet.

For trade to work, everything needs to line up just right: the time, the place, the amounts, and both people have to want what the other person is offering.

Alice, Bobby, and Charlie realized that they needed a better way to trade with each other.

2. MONEY

Another boy in Bitville named Niki noticed Alice, Bobby, and Charlie's trading problems.

"We need to use money!" he exclaimed.

"I've heard of money, but how does it work?" Alice wondered.

"Let's say you want your lawn mowed," Niki began. "You could pay Bobby with money even if he didn't want lemonade that day. Then he could save that money to spend another time, or use it to buy something else."

"If we use money, I could sell pictures every day and save up enough to buy a new art set!" said Charlie with glee. "But what should we use as money?"

Bobby picked up a bag of grass clippings. "Could grass clippings be used as money?"

"That won't work," said Niki. "There are too many grass clippings. Grass grows everywhere. We need something that has a limited supply."

Grass money was not going to happen.

"What about cups of lemonade? Could that be money?" asked Alice.

"Lemonade doesn't taste very good after it sits out for a few days, and it's hard to carry around without spilling. We need something that you can carry in your pocket."

Lemonade money would not be a good idea.

The kids thought about what else they might use as money.

Shiny rocks are limited in supply because they are hard to find in the ground, but they aren't all the same. Some are more beautiful and valuable than others, so it's hard to keep track of how much each one is worth.

Bicycles are something that people want, but they are expensive, and you can't start splitting a bike into smaller parts to make change!

Trees give shade and are fun to climb and swing on, but you can't carry them around to give to someone else when you want to buy something.

Flash! An idea popped into Niki's head. "Let's ask Goldie if we can use her metal coin collection as money!"

Goldie's father collected metal coins, and every week he would give Goldie a few coins to add to her own collection. Every coin weighed the same amount.

"If we use metal coin money, we'll know how many coins there are to start, and since Goldie only gets a few extra coins per week, the supply is still pretty limited," Niki said.

Charlie was starting to like this idea. "Metal coins fit nicely in your pocket or a purse, and they don't get spoiled. I could use one coin to buy a cup of lemonade and five coins to have my lawn mowed."

Goldie was happy that everyone wanted to use her metal coins for money.

She traded some of her coins for lemonade, drawings, and lawn mowing, until eventually everyone had some metal coin money of their own.

Things were going really great in Bitville.

3. PAPER

Some of the kids in Bitville saw how much metal money Alice, Bobby, and Charlie were collecting with their businesses, and they thought that was great!

They were inspired to use their own special skills to start businesses and earn metal money for themselves.

Soon enough there were even more businesses in Bitville: Tony taught classes, Jim fixed computers, Lena built cool toys, Sam sold hats, and Dean opened his own BBQ stand.

Eventually everyone in town had their own collection of metal money.

Some kids had more money, and some had less, but that was okay because everybody helped each other in times of need.

Using good money made life better for everyone.

There was one big problem with all of this new metal money though... it was heavy!

Some kids' pockets became so heavy they dragged on the ground. And if you had a hole in your pocket, well, that could cause a lot of problems!

Benny, who was one of the most trustworthy kids in town, came up with a solution.

"I have a safe in my house where we keep very important things. I could keep your metal money in my safe, and then I'll print out certificates for everyone to show how much money they each have."

"You can carry around the paper money, and it won't be so heavy."

Paper money seemed like a strange idea to some of the kids, but because Benny was so trustworthy, everyone agreed to start using it.

In fact, once it caught on, all the kids loved using paper money. It was so much easier to carry around, and everybody knew their metal coins—the real money— were secure in Benny's safe.

They also knew that one paper certificate was always worth one metal coin.

Once again, life in Bitville was improving.

4. PRINTING

As time passed, and everyone in Bitville continued to use paper money, they almost forgot that there were metal coins in a safe at Benny's house.

The coins were the money which they originally picked for its good qualities; paper money was just a fill-in.

When summer came, Benny announced that he was going away to camp, but not to worry, his brother Freddy would be taking care of the safe for now.

Most kids didn't even notice the change.

Freddy started off taking care of the metal coins just like his brother Benny. He would only give out as much paper money as he had coins in the safe.

But Freddy's friend Kenny had a different idea.

Kenny saw how much everybody loved paper money. He thought to himself, "If people love paper money, and they use it to buy things and start businesses, then wouldn't it be better if they had *even more* paper money?"

Kenny didn't understand that paper money was just a fill-in for metal money, which was also just a fill-in for the work that people did in the first place.

You can print more paper money, but you can't print more hard work. That takes time, effort, and energy.

Freddy and Kenny thought they were doing everybody a favor, and it helped that they also got to keep the first batch of freshly-printed paper money for themselves.

At first everything seemed to be going great.

Kids loved having all of this extra money printed. Especially the ones who were friends with Freddy and Kenny, since they got the new money before everyone else.

Alice thought her business was booming. Every day she ran out of cups of lemonade, but there were still more customers with all the extra paper money.

Being a smart businesswoman, she decided to raise the price from one paper bill per cup to two. Now she was making twice as much money!

Alice was excited to imagine all the things she could buy with so much money! But when she tried to buy a drawing from Charlie, she realized his prices had doubled, too!

Alice had more paper money, but she couldn't buy anything more than before.

At the end of the summer, when Benny came back home, he was easily convinced to go along with the money-printing plan.

When the other kids came back from camp, they also noticed that their paper money bought a lot less than it used to.

"Maybe we should just go back to using metal money," Charlie told Benny.

Benny, Freddy, and Kenny liked their endless supply of paper money.

"I don't even have the code to the safe anymore," Benny said. "Just trust us, this is the best idea ever."

This newly-printed paper also changed the way kids saved and spent money.

Instead of saving to buy something nice, every kid knew they had to spend it right away, or else it might be worth even less the next day.

A cup of lemonade that used to cost only one paper bill eventually ended up costing 100 paper bills! Sometimes you would even find paper money being swept in the street because it was worth so little.

Things were not going well in Bitville.

5. BITCOIN

One day a new boy moved to Bitville. He called himself Satoshi, but nobody knew much else about him.

Satoshi noticed that the kids in Bitville were not happy about more and more paper money being printed each day.

Satoshi thought to himself, "What if we could make a new kind of money that is limited in supply like metal money, but it isn't heavy? Then everyone could carry it around for themselves, without having to trust anybody to keep it in a safe for them."

He sat down and started brainstorming. He asked some of the other kids for their advice, too. Niki knew a lot about how money worked, and another boy in town named Al was very good at math.

After months of planning, Satoshi shared his idea with everyone. He called it **Bitcoin.**

It was very complicated, but he tried to explain it simply.

"There will be a big chart in the middle of town that shows how much money every person has. Every day, we'll meet here and update the chart with any changes of who gave some of their money to somebody else."

"Everyone will also keep their own copy of the chart, so nobody can come when no one's looking and make fake changes. This way we can all have our own money just by keeping track of this chart, and we can all make sure nobody is adding any new money."

	1	2	3	4
Alice	16	14		
Bobby	8	9		
Charlie	5	11		
Niki	43	38		

At first, most of the kids were not interested in this new Bitcoin money.

"It will never work!" said one girl.

"If it doesn't come from Freddy and Kenny, it's not real money!" said one of Freddy and Kenny's good friends.

But Satoshi and his friends continued to improve his invention. Instead of using a written chart, Satoshi figured out how to make Bitcoin work as an app.

Some kids wondered why they should trust Satoshi to be in charge of the money. They barely even knew him!

Satoshi explained that nobody needed to trust him at all. Since everyone had their own app, they could check the code themselves without needing to trust him or anyone else!

Each person could run their own app to keep track of the Bitcoin themselves and make sure nobody was cheating.

When they realized that nobody was in charge of this new money, not even Satoshi, some of the kids in Bitville got very excited and started using Bitcoin.

Bitcoin began to catch on. Some kids wanted to spend it, some wanted to save it, and some wanted to use it to send money to friends who lived far away.

The kids who didn't use Bitcoin began to realize that their paper money kept losing value because more and more was being printed. But Bitcoin money kept gaining value because the app was designed so that everyone could verify that there was a limited amount.

It was even more limited than Goldie's metal coins, since she would get a few new coins each week.

Kids loved Bitcoin because, as an app, it was easy to carry around. Bitcoins were very durable, too. You could make a backup to keep them safe.

They could be spent in various amounts: three Bitcoins for a steak, six Bitcoins for a hat, or half a Bitcoin for a cup of lemonade. And every single Bitcoin was worth the same as every other Bitcoin.

Bitcoin was running smoothly when, to everyone's surprise, Satoshi suddenly announced that he was leaving Bitville. "My family is moving on to other things in a different town," he declared, before mysteriously disappearing.

Nobody has seen or heard from him since.

Some kids wonder if "Satoshi" was even his real name.

The good thing was that Bitcoin was just fine with Satoshi gone. Since everyone was running their own app, they didn't need him anymore to make Bitcoin work.

It seemed that Bitville had finally found a good money: Bitcoin money.

6. COPIES

For everyone who was using Bitcoin money, things were going great!

But not everybody was happy.

Freddy and Kenny didn't like that kids were starting to use a different kind of money. Their freshly-printed paper money quickly lost its value.

First Freddy and Kenny tried to deny that Bitcoin could ever work, but that clearly wasn't the case.

Then they thought of another idea. What if they made their own copy of Bitcoin that they were in charge of?

"Bitcoin isn't really money, only we can make money. But the technology is very interesting, so we've made our own money called Fred-Coin!" Freddy announced with great enthusiasm.

But the kids in Bitville weren't buying it. They remembered the last time they trusted Freddy and Kenny to take care of their money. The whole point of Bitcoin was that you didn't need to trust anybody.

Other kids also tried to make their own copies of Bitcoin. There was ABC-Coin and XYZ-Coin. There was Bitcoin-Big and Bitcoin-Small.

Many of these coins had the same problem as paper money; in order to use them, you had to trust the person who made them.

"You don't need to run your own app, you can trust me! I won't make the same mistakes as Freddy and Kenny," was often heard.

But by this time, most kids liked to be able to verify their own money with their own app.

They liked the real Bitcoin.

And besides, if everyone created their own money, wouldn't that be just as bad as when too much paper money was printed? It would be even worse!

These Bitcoin copies were not good money.

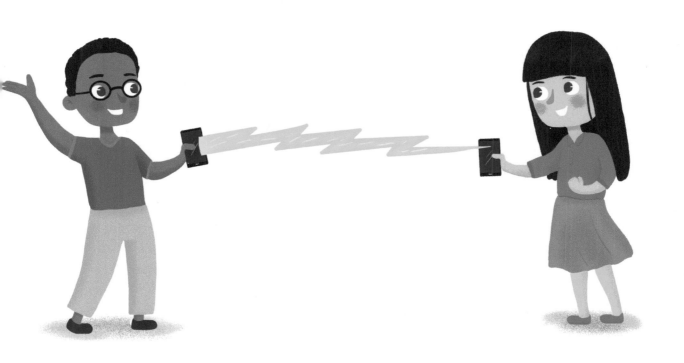

Some kids complained that Bitcoin was too slow, but Lizzie and Lollie, two really smart kids, worked on a way to make Bitcoin lightning fast!

When most kids in Bitville used Bitcoin, life improved for everyone. They could save money or build businesses easily because Bitcoin was fair and reliable.

With Bitcoin as their money, the future looked bright for Bitville.

EPILOGUE

The kids in Bitville wanted to make their lives better by working hard and providing goods and services for each other.

Bobby knew that by mowing lawns, he could make life better for all the kids who wanted their lawns mowed, and in exchange they would make his life better by giving him something he wanted. Alice could get the goods and services that she wanted by providing lemonade to other kids.

They soon realized that direct trade and barter can only work if everything matches up: the time, the place, the amounts, and the wants of both sides. Most of the time a tool is needed to make trading easier. That tool is money. With money, you can save, exchange, and easily keep track of value.

But not everything can be used as money.

Your time and energy is very important because it is limited. So, when you trade your time and energy for money, you need to make sure that the money you're getting in return is limited and valuable as well.

The kids from Bitville searched for the best kind of money. It had to be durable, portable, uniform, divisible, and limited in supply.

They tried many options, but in the end, they discovered that Bitcoin was the best money.

ABOUT THE AUTHOR

Rabbi Michael Caras studied Jewish law and ethics at Yeshiva Ohr Tmimim in Kfar Chabad, Israel. He currently lives in Albany, NY where he teaches about Judaism, digital media, and technology at a Jewish day school.

Since 2017 he has been interested in Bitcoin, making connections between technology, spirituality, economics, and ethics.

thebitcoinrabbi@gmail.com
thebitcoinrabbi.com
twitter.com/thebitcoinrabbi

ACKNOWLEDGMENTS

This book was greatly inspired by the works of others, in particular:

How an Economy Grows and Why it Crashes, Peter D. Schiff
Bitcoin: A Peer-to-Peer Electronic Cash System, Satoshi Nakamoto
The Bitcoin Standard: The Decentralized Alternative to Central Banking, Saifedean Ammous
Shelling Out: The Origins of Money, Nick Szabo

Thank you to family and friends who reviewed
and gave feedback on early drafts of this book:
Jonathan Caras, Harvey & Joanne Caras, Mendel Shepherd,
Pierre Rochard, Michael Goldstein, Max Hillebrand

CPSIA information can be obtained
at www.ICGtesting.com
Printed in the USA
BVHW050953170920
589014BV00004B/22